Contact Information
https://Neatbooks4u.com; Arnetha@Neatbooks4u.com;
1 786 488-4792

Illustrations by
PeppermintminusWaffles follow on Instagram

Pictures Modified-Ace Printing
1 305 430-8300

Art Rework and Layout by GMOSS Designs, LLC

Sometimes Here, There and Everywhere is: (1) Children's Fiction (2) Poetry (3) Positive Social Skills (4) Critical Thinking (5) Inspirational (6) Hilarious (7) Rhythm (8) Repetition (9) Conflict Resolution/Reconciliation

Printed in the United States of America

Sometimes Here, There and Everywhere

Dedicated to Ary

On a cool Saturday evening before dark, Ary arrived at Mema's house. After looking around she asked, "Where is DJ?" Auntie Neat said, "He has already left for the day." Ary replied, "DJ is never here, when I'm here." Auntie Neat said, "He was here, but you were there." "I was there at my Gema's house" said Ary. Even though she was sadden DJ had left from here to there, Ary said, "I love hanging out with my Gema."

Suddenly Auntie Neat was inspired to write about Ary. She titled the book, *Sometimes Here, There and Everywhere*. Auntie felt sad since it took her a long time to finish the book. So Auntie read the storybook to Ary while she was still a little girl. Ary laughed and laughed. After that Ary would ask over and over again, "Auntie where is my book where is my book?" Auntie kept saying, "I'm working on it I'm working on it." Auntie needed to re-read the book for corrections. Finally Ary stopped asking about *Sometimes Here, There and Everywhere* storybook. Six to seven years later, Auntie Neat finished, re-wrote and now presents *Sometimes Here, There and Everywhere*!

Book dedicated to Ary with much love from Auntie Neat.

Sometimes Here, There and Everywhere is recommended for early learners through third grade, older elementary to secondary children with reading or some learning disabilities.

While riding with Grandma Gema, Ary thought about the time she almost frightened Mema, her other grandma, out of her skin. "Oh my God" Ary had said. Mema did not know she was in the house. Ary had walked into the house without greeting her grandma.

On that very day Ary learned the importance of having good manners. Ary learned to never walk into the house without greeting family like daddy, momma, Mema, Gema, granddaddy, brother, sister and cousin.

She learned to greet someone is saying words like hello, hi, good morning or good afternoon. The person coming into the room should speak, because it is having good manners.

Ary says, "When I or someone else gets ready to leave, it is polite to say something like goodbye, see you later, so long, or after while crocodile." Polite is to have good manners.

So Gema finally arrived at Mema's house. Mema
knew they were coming and heard a knocking
on the door. Peeping through the small door
hole she saw them. Mema opened the
door wide and went outside.

Ary said, "Hey Mema." Mema said, "Hey Ary."
Together they swayed without delay
in a huggable way.

Mema said, "Hi Gema!"
Gema said, "Hi Mema!"

Mema asked without speaking too fast,
"Gema..... how..... are..... you..... doing.....?"
Gema answered slowly,
"I'm..... doing..... good.....!"

Gema asked without speaking too fast,
"Mema..... how..... are..... you..... doing.....?"
Mema answered slowly,
"All.....is..... well.....!"

Gema then said to Mema,
"Here's your package."
"Thank you", said Mema.

Ary said, "Bye bye Gema"
Gema said, "Bye bye Ary."

They parted with a hug
and a goodbye kiss.

Then Ary went inside.
Auntie Neat into the living room she came.
Who came? Auntie Neat, She came
and said, "Hi Ary."
Ary said, "Hi Auntie Neat."
"Hi Auntie Neat," she said.

Who said? She said.
Ary said, "Hi Auntie Neat!"

Ary gave Auntie Neat a kiss on the cheek.
Guess what
Guess who
wear big big shoes on her big big feet?
Yes! Auntie Neat
wear big big shoes
to fit her big big feet!
Ary said, "I love my Auntie Neat's big big feet
big big shoes and all!"

Then Ary walks through the house for DJ
looking here
looking there and
looking everywhere.
She did not find DJ here.
She did not find DJ there.
She did not find DJ anywhere.

Ary looked high.
Ary looked low.
She asked herself, "Where did DJ go?"

Ary asked Auntie Neat, "Where is DJ?
Is he with JJ?"
Auntie replied, "No, DJ is not with JJ.
DJ left before today.
He did not stay."

Ary asked, "Where is DJ where is DJ?"
Auntie replied, "He had to go home.
He is not alone."

Ary's responses were, "Oh my God!
DJ is never here, when I'm here!"
Before Auntie Neat could finish her sentence,
Ary said, "Excuse me Auntie, but when DJ is here
I'm sometimes here, there and everywhere!"

Auntie Neat said, "That's right Ary!
You are sometimes, here, there and everywhere!"
Ary giggles and laughs out loud!

After Ary giggles and laughs out loud she said,
"When I'm there at my Gema's house
doing this and that
DJ is here at my Mema's house."

Ary said, "When I'm there at my daddy's house
doing this and that
DJ is here at my Mema's house."

Ary said, "When I'm there at my momma's house
doing this and that
DJ is here at my Mema's house."

Ary laughs and said,
"I'm sometimes here, there and everywherere!

Ary said, "There are many places I go
like the school
learning all I should
reading
writing
math
science
social studies
physical education
music and
art.

While at the school
I'm sometimes here, there and everywhere!"

Like the church
learning all I should in
Sunday School
Vacation Bible School
Bible Study
children's classes
choir practices
usher board meetings
children's clubs and
children's activities.

While at the church
I'm sometimes here, there and everywhere!

Like the park
playing very hard
swinging
sliding
skating
running
jumping
kicking and
swimming.

While at the park
I'm sometimes here, there and everywhere!

Like the store
shopping
from one to the next
no time to rest
looking for the best
shoes
clothes
book-bag
phone
tablet and
games.

While at the store
I'm sometimes here, there and everywhere!

Like the doctor's office
for a physical, shot or flu.

. Like the dentist
opening my mouth.
I open it wide
and I don't cry!

Like the eye doctor
their shiny light
twinkling in my eyes.

While at the doctors' offices,
I'm sometimes here, there and everywhere!

Like the movies
I choose my seat
closer to the front
further to the back
somewhere in the middle
I chose and sat.

Eating my popcorn
can't hardly wait
for the movie to get on the way
without delay.

I love funny, cartoon, family and animal movies.

While at the movies
I'm sometimes, here, there and everywhere!

Like out of town
out of town I go.

I travel by
car
bus
train
boat
and
airplane.

While out of town
I'm sometimes here, there and everywhere!

Ary said, "Auntie Neat I'm sometimes,
here, there and everywhere.

Sometimes I'm at Gema, Mema, daddy and momma's
house. Sometimes I'm at school, church, the park, shopping, doctors' offices, movies and out of town."

Ary said, "Auntie Neat, I'm Sometimes here, there, and
everywhere." She said, who said? Ary said,
"The next time I'm at Mema's house looking
for DJ and he is not here
I will remember, like me

DJ is sometimes here, there and everywhere!"

Ary hears the door open
"Hello Auntie Mema, I'm back," yelled DJ!

Ary said, "DJ is now here, like me"
and runs to see her cousin, DJ
who is like Ary and like you too.

Sometimes Here, There and Everywhere!

Author/Minister Arnetha Thomas highlights of up-coming and revised published works & projects.

Beautiful as a Butterfly fiction children's storybook currently under revision for animation or possibly screenplay. Filled with dancing and singing. Then DJ says, "I have a big day tomorrow, peace-out!" Scene 2 Caterpillar dances while lying on his green leaf. More to come!

Peer Mediation an awesome process of trained peers helping their peers to peacefully resolve their conflicts reaching "Win/win" resolutions for all parties involved. Some titles of conflict cases are: "Rumors Fly, Stay Out My Face, Bump, Bump, Bump, He/Say-She/Say, Over a Boy, Yelling in the Hallway, Dirty Looks, and The Unknown Lick." Similar to the titles of the new/old re-runs of the Perry Mason Show. Peer Mediation tittles are not fiction, but real. Stay tune for more.

Visit website www.neatbooks4u.com to learn about character Bella. She was the focus in the series of "Get Through, Going Through Life book on blogtalkradio.com/neatbooks.

See website for free resources like templates to encourage participation in Bible Study & Prayer Meeting.

Look forward to Author Arnetha White Paper on Restorative Justice (RJ) Practices a Paramount Community Approach to Building & Mending Relationships.

CPSIA information can be obtained
at www.ICGtesting.com
Printed in the USA
BVHW020937111021
618669BV00022B/652